LEVI'S
LOST CALF

Amanda Radke

Illustrated by Michelle Weber

ISBN: 1463514425
ISBN-13: 9781463514426
Library of Congress Control Number: 2011908705

LEVI'S LOST CALF

A real-life cowboy adventure
written just for you!

For Daddy, my hero.
For Mom, my biggest fan.
For my sisters, my spice in life.
And for Tyler, my best friend.
This cowgirl loves you all.
—Amanda

LEVI'S LOST CALF

Written by Amanda Radke

Illustrated by Michelle Weber

RISE AND SHINE!

It's fall roundup time on the ranch! My name is Levi, and I
live along a dusty, dirt road in the country with my family.
Today, we are up bright and early to bring the mama cows
and their baby calves home from the pasture in preparation
for winter. Although snow will soon be on the way, it's
going to be hot working cattle today! We better hurry
up and get ready to go before the sun comes up.
Will you saddle up and come along for the ride?
I will show you the cowboy way!

The first thing every good cowboy needs is a trusty horse and a loyal cattle dog. When I was little, I had to ride along with Dad, but now that I'm big and strong, I always partner up with my favorite horse, Pepper, and best pal, Gus.
I hear Dad calling; it's time to ride out.
We better hit the trail.

GIDDY UP; LET'S GO!

Wasn't it a fun ride watching the sun come up? What a beautiful day God has blessed us with. Now, the first thing we have to do is count the cows and calves. Like Noah's Ark, the pairs are grouped together.

MOOOOOOO!

These cows are getting restless; they are ready to go home! But, wait! I think one calf missing.

"Umm, Dad? Where's Little Red, my favorite baby heifer? She's nowhere to be found!

DON'T WORRY, DAD!

I will take Pepper and Gus and go look for her!"

Will you help me search for the baby heifer calf too?

Let's get started. We will head back to the barnyard first.
She is not by the barn. It's just a proud peacock prancing to
and fro over there. Let's look inside.

She is not inside the barn up in the hay loft.
What's up there? It's only a napping kitty cat
curled up catching some

She is not in the shelter belt. Do you hear that rustling? There is a plump, golden pheasant waddling in the shade under the trees.

She is not in the garden, but Mom would be mad to see that fuzzy, fluffy bunny rabbit snacking on her fresh cabbage.

SHOO, BUNNY, SHOO.

She is not in the corn field, but do you see that rowdy raccoon grabbing ears of corn over there? Hey, that corn is for the cows, pal!

SKEDADDLE, YOU LITTLE RASCAL!

She is not in the grain bin. It's just a hungry squirrel nibbling on feed in there. Our ranch sure feeds a lot of hungry animals, doesn't it? Seeing wildlife is a fun part of living in the country; you never know what you might find on the ranch!

In our hunt for Little Red, we have found a proud peacock prancing; a sleepy kitty cat napping; a plump, golden pheasant waddling; a fuzzy, fluffy bunny snacking; a rowdy raccoon grabbing corn; and a hungry squirrel nibbling. Where in the world is Little Red? She is nowhere to be found! Dad trusts us to find her.

THINK, THINK, THINK.

Even Pepper is starting to get worried.
What should we do?
What would a cowboy do?

Boy, it's a warm fall day today! The sun is getting hot.
I could use lunch and a nap. My tummy is rumbling, and
I'm tired, but we are responsible for finding Little Red.
The animals always come first on a family ranch,
no matter what.

Hey, wait! I have an idea!
Do you think Little Red wanted a nap, too?
I think I know where she is!
Let's ride back out to the pasture, and fast!

HEEEYAAAW!

Whew! There she is!
Just like I thought; Little Red is taking a nap.
I knew it all along, of course. I wasn't worried at all!
Wake up, Little Red. Your mama is wondering
where you are.

Do you hear her calling?

MOOOOOOO!

Time to go back to the herd. Dad is waiting for all of us to
return. Let's move her back toward the cows.

Little Red is back with her mama now, and the baby
heifer gets a big, wet, sloppy kiss.

SMOOOOOOOOCH!

Ahh, man! My mom still does that when I come home, too!
The cow is so happy to have found her baby, and so am I!
I knew we could do it!

As soon as Little Red and her mama run into the corral,
fall roundup on the ranch is complete!
Good work, cowboy!

HURRAY!

The sun is setting, but before we finish our hard work for
the day, we must feed and water the cows, the horses, and
our dog, Gus. Taking care of the animals is an important
part of ranch life, and doing what's right is just the cowboy
way. Now that the animals are eating, it's our turn!
Let's head inside for our own cowboy feast.

As the day comes to an end and the supper dishes are put away, I kiss my parents good night and head to bed. Before I lay my head to rest, I remember to say my prayers.

Thanks, God, for my pals, Gus and Pepper; for the warm sunshine; and for the green grass and the golden crops. Thank you for the playful, hungry, busy creatures living on our ranch. Thank you for helping us find Little Red today, and for the new cowboy friends I made on the adventure. Most of all, thank you for the food on my plate, my nice, warm bed, and my loving family. Life is good, and I am blessed. Amen.

Good night, cowboys and cowgirls.

SWEET DREAMS.

FIRE UP THE GRILL FOR A COWBOY COOKOUT!

Before enjoying your cowboy cookout, be safe! Get permission first and have an adult supervise you in the kitchen at all times. Watch out for sharp knives and hot objects. The publisher and author disclaim any liability from any injury that might result from the use, proper or improper, of the recipes contained in the book.

ENJOY A SWEET TREAT!

BRUSH UP ON YOUR COWBOY VOCABULARY.

Calf - A baby cow who nurses its mom for approximately six months.

Cattle - A group of cows.

Corral - A big pen to work and sort the cattle through.

Field - A plot of soil where crops, like corn, beans, wheat, and oats, are planted.

Harvest - In the fall, a machine called a combine cuts, threshes, and collects the crops.

Grain - What ranchers feed to cattle when the grass becomes dormant in the winter.

Grain Bin - A large storage unit for the crops.

Grazing - What cattle do when they are chomping on green grass in the summer.

Hay Loft - Grass is cut, dried, and baled into rolls for winter feeding and stored here.

Heifer - A girl cow. The boy cow is called a bull.

Pasture - Rolling hills of grass where cattle graze and spend their summers.

Ranch - A place where cattle, sheep, dogs, horses, and people live and work.

Roundup - The time of year when cattle are brought home to be fed and protected from the harsh winter weather.

Shelter Belt - A group of trees planted by ranchers to shield the cattle from the wind and offer a place for wildlife to live.

WALK LIKE A COWBOY
TALK LIKE A COWBOY

MEET THE COWGIRLS BEHIND THE BOOK.

Author Amanda Radke is a rancher who raises cattle with her family at Nolz Limousin in Mitchell, SD. When she's not busy on the ranch, she's working as a freelance writer and motivational speaker, focused on grilling up healthy, delicious beef.

Illustrator Michelle Weber is a painter, graphic designer and ranch wife from Lake Benton, MN. She, along with her husband, Jesse, raise Red Angus cattle and own Weber Land and Cattle.

Amanda's ranch was the inspiration for "Levi's Lost Calf," and many of the paintings in the book feature the animals found in and around her pastures.

Made in the USA
Lexington, KY
18 August 2011